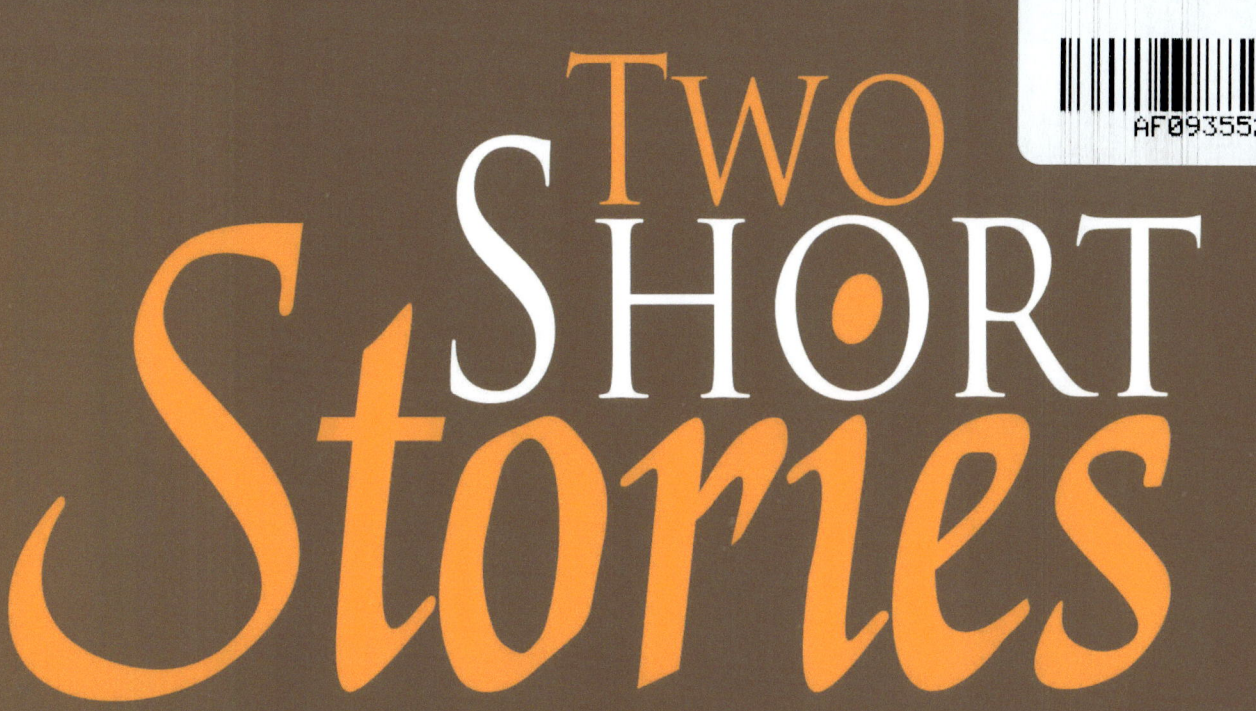

Two Short Stories

Mrs. Canopca and The Vivaldi Bird

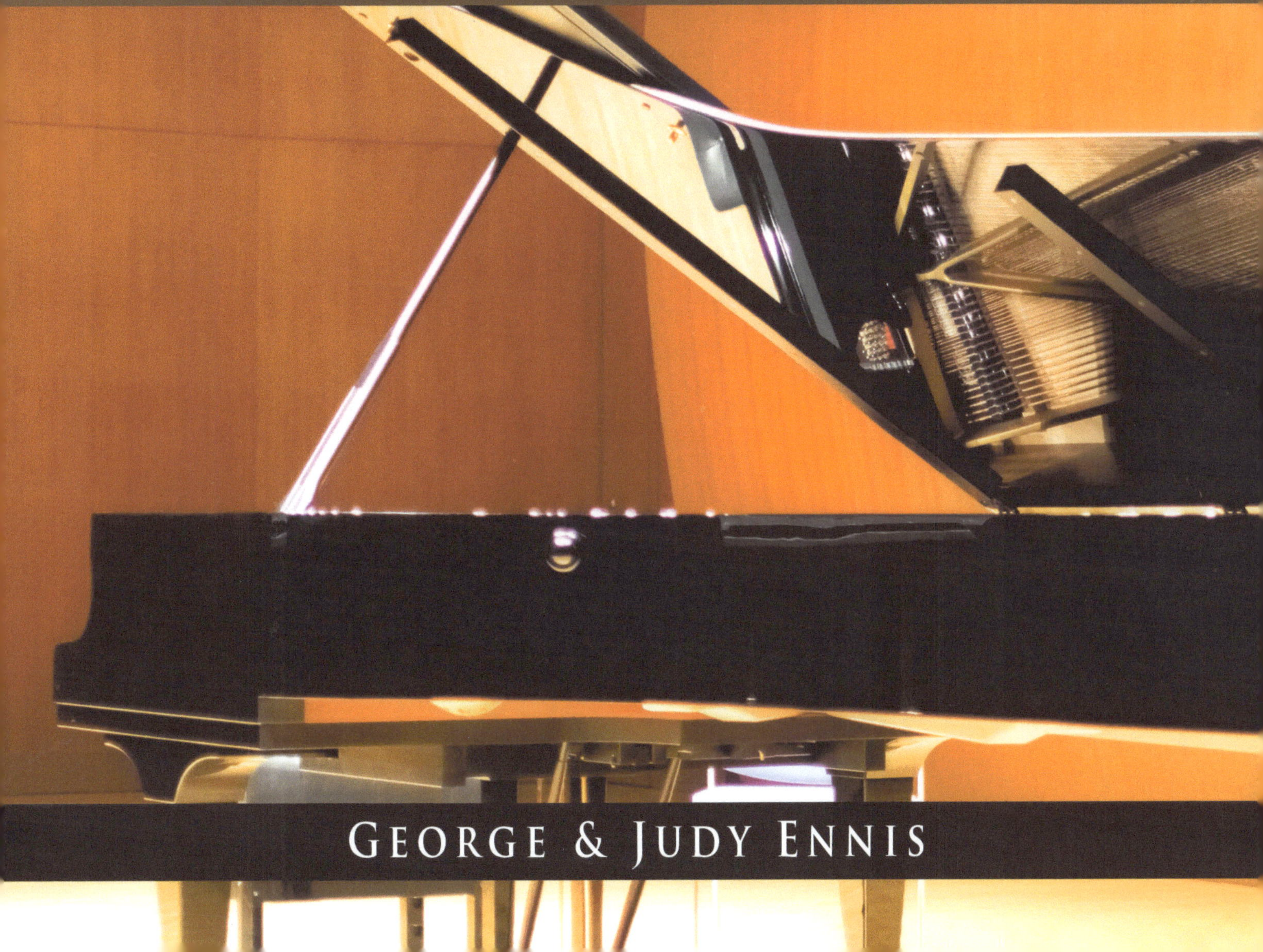

George & Judy Ennis

Two Short Stories

GEORGE ENNIS ; JUDY ENNIS

Two Short Stories
Copyright © 2024 by George & Judy Ennis

ISBN: 979-8895310403 (hc)
ISBN: 979-8895310397 (sc)
ISBN: 979-8895310410 (e)

All rights reserved. No part of this publication may be reproduced, distributed, or transmitted in any form or by any means, including photocopying, recording, or other electronic or mechanical methods, without the prior written permission of the publisher and/or the author, except in the case of brief quotations embodied in critical reviews and other noncommercial uses permitted by copyright law.

The views expressed in this book are solely those of the author and do not necessarily reflect the views of the publisher, and the publisher hereby disclaims any responsibility for them.

Writers' Branding
(877) 608-6550
www.writersbranding.com
media@writersbranding.com

I would like to dedicate this book to my wife who is a terrific typist. Mrs. Canopca

Mrs. Canopca

Mrs. Canopca was late to her first rehearsal at St. John's. She had turned left instead of right, and she drove around the unfamiliar neighborhood until she reached the back of the building. On leaving her car she ran. Her high heels clicked up the steps of the church. Mrs. Canopca had just reached 70 and was very proud that she could run short distances. She had reason to be proud for she was tall and elegant. She was easily recognizable on stage for her hair was a shining silver. Mrs. Canopca entered the foyer and saw a maintenance man dusting a statue. He came forward to greet her and held out his hand, but she darted past him into the sanctuary. She was sorry, but she was too busy for people like that. She could not waste time with the hired help when she was in such a hurry.

She joined the other ladies of the choir and prepared her music for the Bethlehem Cantata. Considering her ability and stature, this was her due. Mrs. Canopca was a gifted artist who moved in a circle of other artists of her kind and caliber. She had an exceptional voice even from childhood and usually took the principal choral parts.

Mrs. Canopca's thoughts were soon interrupted for the maintenance man came down the aisle behind her putting music books in the pews. She eyed him suspiciously. What a funny little monkey he was. His face, neck and hands were wrinkled which betrayed possibly an Indian origin. He was dark and possibly Mexican. His ears and nose were too large, his forehead sloped back like some comical Aztec diety. What bothered her most was that he darted around the alter with a dust rag or handkerchief with an air of authority. He was impertinent. Then a curious thing happened. He stepped onto the dais on which the organ was mounted. Mrs. Canopca held her breath. He was only dusting it. Then he slipped onto the bench and adjusted the light. He was preparing the organ for tonight's rehearsal. Then he made a sign to someone behind her, and the doors slowly began to close. Mrs. Canopca was tortured by the ambiguity of his actions. He wiped his hands briskly with the handkerchief, and the entire church fell to an obedient hush.

Mrs. Canopca was so shocked that shivers passed up her spine. The funny little monkey pressed something under a manual and stops jumped out. He extended his fingers over the glowing ivory keys.

The lovely, familiar mordant and four little notes running down the scale filled the church. He was playing the giant of organ pieces. This was her daily bread, the very music that brought her to God's throne. From the very first measures she realized this man was a sublime genius. He had a style that was strangely romantic considering the period it was composed in. His rubato style made her forget the technical aspects. It excited her like a child hearing it for the first time. She had never felt imagery before in listening to baroque works. But now hearing his brilliant pedal work, she was transported into a world of primitive nature just like in the Creation. She heard lions roaring. She was blasted by thunder and lightening. She heard a waterfall crashing on granite. Truly this was the voice of God!

As she watched him from the profile, the wrinkles etched in his face betrayed his thoughtful expressions. If he appeared simian before, now she beheld him as a philosopher. He was darker than she, but this was because he was a Mediterranean or romantic type.

Before she knew it, it was over. In her trance she was not even aware of the climax. When she awoke, the bitter realization of what she had done to him came back to her. She was mortified. The ladies around her were so moved they ran to the organ. They clutched his hands. Some were in tears. Mrs. Canopca was alone in front of the church. She sat in full view of him in a spotlight of shame. She struggled to fight back tears and perspiration. Hers was a monumental faux pas. Now she knew she had to apologize. She swallowed hard. He had played the Toccata and Fugue in D minor by Bach!

Gino Sonetino came to her. The organist was smiling with a broad smile. Mrs. Canopca rose and held out her hand. She even managed a smile. They shook hands. Gino spoke first, "My friends call me Sonny. I would like you to sing the part of Mary in the Bethlehem Cantata."

She answered, "I will consider it a great challenge." He slipped his hand under her right arm and pointed toward the outside doors. They walked up the aisle, through the door and into the garden.

He talked. "The part of Joseph is very difficult. The chorus is composed of the 3 kings and the wise men.

"I am anxious to meet them all!" Monarch butterflies circled and swooped over bushes. "You have set out milkweed, and the sun has done the rest." Mrs. Canopca thought that St. John's was very much like her home and neighbors. Their conversation was so spirited that Mrs. Canopca had completely forgotten her apology.

Sonny confide that this was the first operatic music he had produced. He was very nervous about their opening night.

The Bethlehem Cantata was a great success. They even took it to other churches. Then they performed it in Festival Hall in Arcadia. They made the newspapers. The greatest part of their performance was that Sonny had given her a big hug! Mrs. Canopca repeated his name over and over in her mind; "Gino Sonetino"—to her it sounded like sheer poetry. He was Italian. For Mrs. Canopca Italy was the birthplace of music. The success at Festival Hall brought Sonny a small fortune. Sonny and Mrs. Canopca had many walks in many parks. They shared their past from childhood to maturity. They spoke of how music had enriched their lives. They spoke of their plans for the future, for Bethlehem was going through its fifth performance.

In St. John's Garden in a swirl of butterflies, Sonny asked for her hand, and she accepted the ring. They were married at St. John's. The newspapers had a field day!

> "MARY SNUBS PRODUCER, THEN
> MARRIES HIM 2 MONTHS LATER."

They honeymooned in Italy and lived happily ever after.

The Vivaldi Bird

"Janet, your piano teacher is dying. They took him to Cedars Hospital last night."

Janet had dreaded this moment like no other tragedy in her 18-year-old life. Somehow she hoped Benny would make it through one year at a time if he stopped smoking, but she knew sooner or later it would come. Time passed so quickly. New events came crashing in on her life before the old problems were taken care of. A year ago, in a rage, she ripped her Polonaise to shreds and brought the pieces to Benny, who took her on as his student after retiring from late night concerts and even later parties. Benny ate, drank, and smoked all the time. He played any music without effort, thought Janet. He talked and laughed and kidded her a lot, telling her jokes about pianists' worst moments on the stage. She began to laugh. She remembered vividly Benny talking so quickly, his cigarette fluttered up and down in his mouth. No one else could talk that way. They got on very well together. Her depression subsided, and she enjoyed a springtime of warm, green meadows full of fat, contented animals. She often wondered what she would do when the news came How would she feel? And now it couldn't come at a worse time. She hadn't seen him in a month, and already her pastoral happiness was cracking. This time it was a Vivaldi Pastoral. She ironed out her mistakes each time, but then they came back. Now there were two or three hurdles which she couldn't quite get over: a bunch of 16th notes all at once in the right hand. When Benny played them, they spilled out like clear, bright water on the ground. The last time she tried it, she stumbled. Lightning struck, and she fought back an urge to strike the keys.

Janet collected her Vivaldi, her exercises, and then more and more until she had a five-inch stack of Schirmers and Verlag under her arm. She drove west on Beverly Boulevard hearing all the time Benny's soothing voice talking to her, guiding her, giving her the key to each difficult passage. Once when she was uptight about the Pathetique, he got her to hum the adagio while he sang the bass notes. She found she had a voice. Or he would grab a violin and play around her. The little duets made her shine like the sun. Then she wanted a lesson every day, but Benny said no.

Janet pulled into the hospital parking lot and found a spot since it was still quite early. She pulled her music out of the back seat. It always seemed to be coming apart. Her stride through waiting rooms and corridors was quick and automatic. There were small, dark people in blue uniforms everywhere.

In life and in health Benny was short and roly-poly. His fingers were pudgy but strong, his sleeves covered with white ashes. He had bushy white hair which stood high on his head and a ruddy complexion. His lips were full and sensuous and betrayed an appetite for pleasure. A handkerchief dangled from his breast pocket. Seeing his bright, darting g eyes and high cheekbones for the first time, you knew he was an artist who had traveled everywhere. In his studio were boxes of programs, signed photos, greeting cards and cables in every language. Janet brought him flowers which she planted among the fauns and goddesses of his garden just outside the sliding glass window.

- I'm trying to find Mr. Ben Nye. He was brought in last night.

The receptionist went down her list and found nothing.

- Are you sure you have the right name?

Then Janet recalled his long past which he seldom mentioned and his long full name which he never used.

-David Menachem Ben-Nye.

-Oh, yes, here it is. Are you family?

Janet stood mute, her lips ready to form the lie.

-Look, please let me see him.

-I'm sorry, it's hospital policy to admit only relatives with extremely ill patients.

Janet was not going to take no for an answer, but she didn't know how to fight this. There was an embarrassing silence and then a crescendo of what sounded like German behind her. She wheeled around and saw a role-poly woman, her white hair done up high on her head with tortoise-shell combs. She was the exact replica of Benny, and she seemed angry. The nurses behind the counter made a protest, but the woman waved them away with one staccato word and a sweeping gesture of her hand. She locked arms with Janet, and they were off down a corridor. Now Janet was going to see Benny whether she wanted to or not. The woman continued to speak excitedly in the same bewildering tongue. Janet wondered how the woman knew she had come to see Benny in the first place.

The woman motioned her into a room, and Janet saw her teacher sitting up in bed. She then patted Benny's bed and said, "Zit", and Janet sat down. Benny had grown quite thin and pale. His hair was mostly gone, and a tube was taped to his nose which seemed to hurt him. At the sight of his pupil, his eyes grew warm, luminous, and hopeful. His lips moved, but no words came out. Tears welled up in Janet's eyes. She held up her music and said the first thing that came out of her heart.

-Benny, I don't think I'm going to make it.

Stung by his pupil's remark, his eyes grew cold and dark. Benny raised himself from the hips, seized her hands and held them tightly in his own. He would not let go. Janet cursed herself for her bedside manners and sought to comfort him with a smile. His quick movement caused the entire pile of music to cascade to the floor. Janet made an effort to retrieve it, but Benny held her fast, so the two just sat and looked at each other. The woman who was eating an apple reached down from her chair, retrieved the mess and began to look through it, putting pages back in their right place. Janet looked at the woman apologetically. In five minutes every page was back in its rightful place. The woman looked up suddenly and held out an apple for her. Janet smiled through her tears and shook her head because she could not take it.

Noises came from the corridor outside the room. To Janet's embarrassment, more people came in. They looked like Benny, some short, some tall, some younger and some older. They greeted the woman loudly in the same language. There were embraces as if they came from far away after a long separation. There were some tears and some laughter. They came to Benny's bedside and consoled Janet who was painfully aware that they wanted to take Benny's hand. But there was a special joy in the family in being reunited. Photos came out; food was passed around.

A Rabbi appeared at the door. They rushed to greet him. He wore the large black coat and stiff black hat of his faith. His sideburns were ringlets which twisted down his cheeks. He carried a black box. Janet realized he had not come just to visit. He would do something important, something final. She tried to break Benny's grasp, but he wouldn't let go of her. The Rabbi laid his broad hands on her shoulders as a sign that she should not move. He removed a kidney-shaped pan from the bed table, drew a white cloth from his box and placed it over the table. The Rabbi then replaced his hat with a skull cap, placed a holy object on the cloth and began praying out loud. Janet listened to the verses whose deep resonance stretched back a thousand years. She overcame her fear of not belonging and held tight to her teacher. Just a minute before, she wanted to apologize for being there, break and run, but now she felt pride in being part of them and knew they had accepted her into the family. When the Rabbi finished his prayer, Benny let go.

Late that night Janet sat at her piano and gazed at the keyboard. When she was small, she asked her teacher about the black keys. Mrs. Hiscocks said that they were landmarks to guide her fingers. So Janet thought of them as groups of big mountains and little mountains. The key of C lived just below the little mountain. He was an old friend, and Janet could find him anytime she wanted to. She studied the keys long and hard. They were a landscape that stretched infinitely in both directions. She looked at her hand. This thing that grabbed limbs and peeled bananas could play Vivaldi.

Her hands came down on the first chord of the Vivaldi Pastoral, and she was off on the allegro part. She got through the repeat in fine style and braced for her first hurdle. She slowed slightly, marked her left hand rhythm well and matched a trill to it in her right hand. She was up and over the hurdle. The second time over the trill, she made a small mistake, but it wasn't bad. Then she rested in a moderato: a long series of tall, five-finger chords, that stretched upward like pine trees. Her muscles grew warm and loose like a runner. She embarked on some fast up and down scales in the right hand. She retarded the ending just like Benny and waited half a second before giving the audience the last note. Somehow the piece seemed shorter to her. She was well into the second part. This was her favorite. It was loaded with embellishments, and Janet took great care in making them sound bird-like. A slight mistake in the dove, but her owl and coo coo was even better. She came to the part about the nightingale, her last and biggest hurdle, a fast series of 16th notes all at once in the right hand. She did it smoothly just like clear, bright water poured on the ground. Elated by her ease and ability, she played from sheer delight. She knew there would be no more mistakes. Janet was one of them, hopping buoyantly in the green grass and splashing wildly in the puddles. Janet was the Vivaldi bird.

www.ingramcontent.com/pod-product-compliance
Lightning Source LLC
LaVergne TN
LVHW070445070526
838199LV00036B/694